Duncan Du Wigtow Adventure

By Mary Cowan

Illustrated by Angela Ashton

First published in Great Britain in 2013 by
J&B Print Ltd.
info@jandbprint.co.uk
www.jandbprint.co.uk

ISBN 978-0-9574323-1-4

Printed by
J&B Print
32a Albert Street
Newton Stewart
DG8 6EJ
Tel: 01671 404123

To Dib and Heather

Chapter One

Max the otter stood next to the crumbling wall and admired his best friend. Duncan Dunbar was the coolest friend anyone could ever wish for. Cool clothes, cool hair and the coolest of characters; Duncan had it all.

Max shook with nervous excitement because he knew, from the tell tale signs, that Duncan was about to fart.

Duncan's farts were legendary. Duncan Dunbar, farted fireworks. Real, explosive, light up the sky beasties, that would have impressed Guy Fawkes himself.

Three... two... one... and blast off! The balmy, early summer, early evening sky was transformed into a neck craning stage.

Duncan's display began with a succession of ear splitting bangers, followed by a cacophony of colourful rockets, Roman candles and mortars before spectacularly ending with a magnificent, model line up of Catherine wheels in amazing, awesome colours. Wow!

Max and Duncan closed their
eyes and took mighty sniffs to inhale
and appreciate the aromas of the
firework farts.

"Fweshly mown gwass, wif a hint of wemonade?" guessed Max, nervously.

"Grass? Yes. Lemonade? Mmm, almost," teased Duncan.

"Diet Iwn Bwu? Wif a hint of mint?" Max pleaded.

"Yip! You've got it!" grinned Duncan.

Max sighed. He wished that he was as brave and as confident and as talented as Duncan.

Duncan sighed. He was honoured to have such a loyal, trustworthy and intelligent friend like Max.

But Duncan felt guilty. He secretly longed for a daredevilish friend who was wild, daring, adventurous and exciting. Someone like himself...

But Port William was a village,

full of wonderful characters but lacking in adventurous friends to choose from. Duncan dreamed that one day he would find a second friend to share his adventures with.

Then like a noisy response to his firework farts, he could hear an excited racket of voices approaching.

Some enthusiastic village cyclists were whooping their way over Duncan's humped back bridge towards the farm.

From experience Duncan knew this meant an evening of rowdy disruption. Millie the farmer's wife was entertaining her friends with one of her famous curry and Irn Bru party nights.

Oh yes. At ten o 'clock, well past those pesky children's bedtimes, they would all come squealing, giggling and wobbling their way back to the village. Duncan would be drifting off into a mischief filled dream when he would be rudely awakened.

"I thuppothe we're in for a noithy night Duncan," lisped Max. "You got vewy cwoss the wast time, didn't you. And the time befow that. You fwew wotten fish and old wewies at them, didn't you?"

"Cow pats," announced Duncan.

"No, I don't wemember you fowing cow pats," said Max, scratching his head.

"Cow pats are what we need tonight! Lots of them! Pats that are wonderfully crusty on the outside and gloriously soft and runny in the inside!" grinned Max.

"Cow pats? Are you going to fo

cow pats at them tonight?" Max asked, in amazed disbelief.

"Wait and see, my wee friend!" chuckled Duncan, his eyes twinkling with delight.

By half past nine Duncan and Max had wheelbarrowed dozens of semi-baked cow pats onto the hump backed bridge. Max arranged his in beautifully neat rows while Duncan chucked his like Frisbees, randomly over the pot holed surface of the ancient bridge. The smell they created was not pleasant, especially when some cracked open as they landed.

Right on cue at ten o'clock Duncan and Max heard the start of the shouts and squawks. High as kites, with bellies stuffed with tikka masala and Irn Bru, the mums were singing and the children were squealing.

Way ahead and snaking her way towards the bridge was the mum called Debs, tunelessly singing 'Dancing Queen' at the top of her voice. Unafraid of being seen by Debs, Duncan was cheekily perched on the wall of the bridge.

Debs came wobbling along (because she was waving both hands in the air) screeching, "...young and

sweet only seventeen, oh yeah…oh no! Ahhhh!"

The wheels of her bike had met the cow pats. Debs was catapulted into the air, performing a messy somersault above the bridge before landing with an almighty thud in front of a well amused, satisfied and mischievous troll.

Debs heard the sickening splash of her prized bike landing in the burn. At the exact same moment she found herself staring in disbelief at Duncan. While she slowly turned her head to look at her mangled bike, crashed against the rocks in the burn, Duncan hot footed it back home to his cosy home under the bridge.

When Debs turned her head back
to study Duncan more closely, she
blinked, rubbed her eyes and gaped
at the bridge. There was nobody
there. No strange looking troll.
Nobody. Nothing. Zilch.

Chapter Two

Debs gathered up her sorry state of a bike and began wheeling it home, in a mesmerised stroll. Lagging way behind the others, flashing images of a grinning, cheeky, troll tormented her brain. The others were so excited they had failed to notice Debs was missing and were now singing "Hi Ho Silver Lining".

Of course Debs had laughed at the legend of the Blether Bridge troll with everyone else in the area; the story had been used to attract tourists to the area - a bit like the Loch Ness Monster.

But Debs was an intelligent woman. She had a responsible job working for the council. Intelligent, responsible people did not believe in trolls. But this intelligent, responsible council worker had DEFINITELY come face to face with a real live troll.

Debs drank a huge mug of black coffee then went to bed and half slept with rumbled, troubled, troll filled dreams.

In the morning at their laden kitchen table, two of Debs' eight children were happily reminiscing about the curry and Irn Bru party as they enjoyed crisps, chocolate and fizzy drinks for breakfast.

Neither of their parents noticed the hurried consumption of the forbidden breakfast foods. Dad was behind the newspaper looking exhausted after a late night at the rugby club and Debs was uncharacteristically very quiet, engrossed in laptop search engines.

Feeling slightly sick after their junk food breakfast, Hope and Faith began to gather up the empty packets and wrappers that were the evidence of their unhealthy meal.

"Mum's acting a bit strange," whispered Faith to Hope.

"Too much curry last night. Same every time," replied Hope.

"No, look...she has a kind of glazed look on her face," argued Faith.

"It's just the curry effects; take my word for it. I'm older than you," Hope gloated. (Hope was ten and Faith was eight.)

"She went weird last night after she fell off her bike," said Faith.

"Weird!!" they joked and danced together.

Their giggles were interrupted by Hope's phone mooing.

It was a text message from Grumpy Jock, (known to everyone, apart from himself, as GJ) Millie's husband.

It read ksdjfhiuwrhskfbbskka. (GJ refused to learn how to work a mobile phone, so he just pressed random letters to attract attention.)

"Looks like GJ is ready for us to start work," announced Hope.

"Can we play extreme Pooh sticks on the way there? Puh uh leees?" squeezed Faith.

"Yes, I suppose...but no more expensive stuff thrown in as an experiment," decided Hope.

"Woo hoo! I have a new plan for an indestructible Pooh stick object!" shrieked Faith.

The girls retrieved their bikes and headed to the farm. Every year GJ asked for their help to prepare the calves to be judged at Wigtown Show.

The show was the highlight of the year for local people. It was a huge day out. Farmers entered their animals in competitions to be judged on how good and healthy they looked and there were displays of farm machinery, food marquees and fairground rides. Not to mention all the horses and the show jumping events. Everyone went to Wigtown Show. The weeks before the show were spent preparing for the big day.

As they approached Blether Bridge between their house and the farm, Faith jumped off her bike and began opening her rucksack. Ever since they had been toddlers, they had loved playing Pooh sticks. Invented by Winnie the Pooh, you all threw a twig into the burn, then watched to see whose twig appeared out first at the other side of the bridge.

Except at Blether Bridge. Playing Pooh sticks there was a very mysterious affair because nobody EVER won. For some strange unknown reason, the sticks never appeared out at the other side of the bridge. Not once. Never.

The burn flowed into the sea at the village. Over the years they had been in trouble for throwing in brand new wellies, doughnuts, yellow plastic ducks and messages in bottles. Anything they thought that would not cause pollution to the burn, they had tried, much to Debs' annoyance. But today Faith was convinced she had the answer.

Meanwhile Duncan was playing a newly downloaded and complicated game on his laptop. He had almost got the hang of it when once again, his peace was shattered.

"Hmph. It's that pesky, Pooh stick playing pair again," he grumped. "Will they never realise that they won't ever see their precious Pooh sticks again?"

"I wonder what vey'll twy today Duncan," asked Max.

"I hope its tins of baked beans," Duncan replied. "Or prunes. My firework fuel needs stoking up."

"I fanthy some thawbewwies," Max said, licking his lips.

Up on the bridge, Hope couldn't

work out what her sister was up to. "Faith, WHAT are you doing?"

"Magic glitter! This is so going to work! It will go under the bridge, come out the other side and make beautiful, sparkly burn water," she explained proudly.

"But what if you poison all the fish or it makes them choke? Hope asked angrily.

"It's cool!" Faith replied. "It's special glitter fish food! Glittering Gills Gorgeous Bubble Gum flavoured Sparkling Fish Food," she read from the label on the expensive looking packet. "I bought it online," she added.

Down below, Duncan was poised with his massive fishing net. "Ready Max?"

"Weady Duncan!"

As Duncan became impatient, waiting to trap whatever ridiculous objects they threw in, he heard Max shout, "Ooh, wook Duncan, what is this stuff? It's bweautiful!"

The glittery fish food was

shimmering and sparkling as it bobbed along the surface of the water and slipped its way easily through Duncan's awaiting net.

"Catch it Max!" yelled Duncan.

But the little otter was hypnotised by the amazing glittery colours and just stood and gaped at it.

Duncan was furious!

Faith was ecstatic. "I've won! I've won!" she squeaked in delight. "I've won the ultimate Pooh stick challenge. I am the champion!" she whooped. She then took out her phone and began to film the sparkling evidence. Hope gazed in stunned disbelief. After years of failing to watch something reappear at the other side of the bridge, her annoying little sister had succeeded.

As Faith filmed, she shouted excitedly, "Look Hope! There's an otter! He is just sooo cute!"

Hope stared and as Faith continued to film the otter and the glitter, Max turned to look straight at them, chuffed to have been described as cute.

"He's smiling at us," laughed Hope, "keep filming!"

"Wook Duncan! I'm a filmsta! These giwls fink I'm cute and vey're smiwing at me," he said bashfully.

"He's dancing!" Hope shouted in delight.

"Never mind the dancing,"

muttered Faith, "I'm sure he just spoke!"

Then suddenly, a large purple net appeared from under the bridge and scooped up the talking, dancing, filmstar otter.

"He's been captured!" gasped Hope, just as her phone mooed loudly.

hjhfsjkhfkshfskdjhaskjh read the message. "It's GJ again," said Hope, "We'd better go right now."

"But the otter!" cried Faith. He's been caught by a fisherman or someone. We need to check he's OK."

"He'll be fine! Probably a wildlife ranger doing some studies. We have to go. GJ will be waiting and you know how patient he is - not!"

Unconvinced by her sister's assurance, Faith decided she would

venture to the strictly out of bounds
territory of under the bridge on her
way back from the farm.

Chapter Three

GJ half smiled at the girls as they panted up the hill towards the farm. Millie stood with armfuls of old towels, brushes and the coconut scented cow shampoo. It was bath time for the calves.

This year's show calves were reluctant bathers and were even

more reluctant to be taken walks on their special halters. However after an hour, Hope's calf, Primrose, had moved a few metres, although not in the direction Hope wanted her to go.

Faith's calf Tilly however was determined it was going nowhere, no matter how much she gently tugged and cajoled it.

"It's early days," said Millie. "Lots of time left yet. Come into the kitchen for some juice and cake. There might even be some Irn Bru left." They sat down in the friendly kitchen while Millie cut the chocolate cake.

"I have a cool video to show you, Millie," said Hope cheerily.

"Oh what a cutie!" agreed Millie as she watched the otter video. Before the video ended, Millie began pouring water into glasses of orange squash while the girls watched the video to the end. Faith had captured the moment where the purple net had swept up the otter. Unwittingly, she had also filmed Duncan operating the net.

The girls had an unexpected round of a game they often played, called 'Who can open their eyes and mouths the widest?' They stared in disbelief at each other for a long three seconds. Then they bolted out of the kitchen, leaving a confused Millie standing with two glasses of orange squash in her hands.

Meanwhile, Duncan had calmed down. A bit. He was still cross with Max for not catching the glitter and for showing off in front of those pesky Pooh sticker girls.

"That glitter would have looked really good gelled into my hair," he huffed. "Or stuck to the pockets of my jeans. Would have looked nice stuck to the wallpaper too. It would have glowed in the dark probably," he added.

"I'm weawwy, weawwy sowwy Dunky Wunky," apologised Max. "I twied my best to catch it. It just dazzled me so much, I couldn't. I've witten a poem all about it. Wisten."

"No, I'm not wistening...listening," Duncan gruffed, "I'm going shopping!" And he grabbed his scooter and disappeared.

When he said shopping, what he actually meant was bin hoking. Duncan got most of his shopping from Millie's three wheelie bins. He did bin hoke in the village when he could, but transporting his shopping home could be tricky. Millie's bins though were usually sufficient. Finding out of date food, old clothes and pieces of furniture bargains was what Duncan thrived on. Food that was only a day past it's sell by date, clothes that were barely a month out of fashion and chipped wooden furniture; Millie ditched the lot. Debs said her middle names were probably Dee Clutter.

Yes, bin hoking was always guaranteed to lift Duncan out of a bad mood. Max said it was retail therapy - whatever that meant.

As he scooted along at a furious pace, he frowned as he saw The Peskies cycling hurriedly towards him. *Time to hide in the ditch or behind the hedge*, he thought;

contemplating for just a second or two too long, which option would be the quickest.

He dismounted his scooter and was just about to chuck it over the hedge and launch himself into the ditch, when he heard the words he had dreaded hearing all his life.

"It's him!! Oh my goodness!! There he is!! It's the troll from the video!!" yelled Hope.

"He has a scooter! He... is... on... a... scooter," squealed Faith.

"A troll on a scooter," breathed Hope.

The girls had leapt off their bikes and were shaking

with nervous excitement.

"Do you think he might be dangerous?" whispered Faith.

"I don't know! Let's approach him cautiously," suggested Hope.

It was decision time for Duncan. He had come dangerously close to being spotted many times, but this was for real. True, he had teased Debs, but knew he could disappear quickly and leave her stunned. No, this was serious.

Duncan's greatest fear was being captured and being kept in captivity. He was afraid of being put in a zoo or a circus and of being ogled at by paying, laughing spectators. He feared living a life away from Max and his beautiful bridge home and from his idyllic trick playing lifestyle in the rolling countryside beside the sea.

And of course he had let the troll world down into the bargain. He had been spotted. Not an 'oops, nearly got spotted', but a big fat sickening oops.

Duncan stared at the girls. The girls stared back. Hope attempted a faint smile. To return the smile or not, thought Duncan. Could he run faster than them? He might escape today, but would the Pesky Pair organise teams of intrepid troll detectives to track him down?

He closed his eyes slowly and swallowed hard. Where was the brave, adventurous Duncan? Could this be the beginning of his greatest adventure ever? The greatest, most enormous, mind blowing experience?

Chapter 4

Duncan swallowed hard and decided to go for it.

Both girls were now grinning broad, beaming, smiley smiles. Duncan grinned back.

"Good afternoon girls! How lovely to meet you in person at last," ventured Duncan.

"Em yes, you too," agreed Faith, " I like your scooter; our friend at the farm used to have one just like that, when

he was smaller," Faith rambled.

"Are you a real troll? Are you the troll that's rumoured to live near here? Where do you live?" asked Hope in awe.

"Bit thick your sister, is she? Bit of a numpty? Duncan joked. "Well I'm not a kangaroo or a tree frog or a Jack Russell am I? And eh, where do I live? Du-oh! Where do all trolls live? In skyscrapers? In the dentist's waiting room? At the post office? Down the toilet? I live under a bridge of course; Blether Bridge with Max."

"Max?" asked Faith.

"My otter friend whose great, great ancestor was Mij," declared Max proudly.

"Not the Mij in Ring of Bright Water?" exclaimed Hope.

"She's real sharp your sister, isn't she?" teased Duncan.

"So what's your name? I'm Faith and this is Hope," went on Faith.

"Duncan. Duncan Dunbar of the mighty Mochrum Dunbar clan" proclaimed Duncan as he stuck out his chest.

"Wow!" chorused the girls. It is a real honour to meet you," said Faith.

Duncan thought quickly. He was about to ask them to keep a secret with a stranger. He had to choose his words carefully. Honesty was the best policy he decided.

"Yes, you really are honoured," he said. "You are the only humans to ever have met me."

"Wow!" chorused the girls again.

"I have avoided humans all my life you see as I'm afraid they would find me amusing and lock me up like a convict in a cage in a zoo or a circus," his voice trailed as he theatrically put his hand on his brow.

"Oh no! That would be awful! You can't be kept locked up!" Faith agreed.

Bingo! thought Duncan. They are falling for my true sob story.

"I hear you coming onto my bridge all the time and I have always wanted to meet you because you sound so much fun, but I have never introduced myself before as I was scared you would tell the grown ups and I would end up on the TV news and be put in the zoo and ..."

"Oh Duncan! Don't worry," said Hope, "We won't tell the grown ups about you," she assured him and reached out and stroked his hairy little arm.

"You can trust us!" agreed Faith, "And some of our friends," she chanced.

"Oh thank you!" breathed Duncan with a sigh of relief. "I was sure I could trust you!"

"So where are you scooting to?" asked Faith.

"Oh just out for some exercise," Duncan fibbed, "I'm going to head home now."

The new friends then cycled and scooted back to the bridge together. The girls bombarded Duncan with questions and as he answered, his thoughts were full of the adventure opportunities that having human friends might bring. The girls' heads were full of just wow thoughts that they had befriended a real live troll.

Chapter Five

The girls swapped phone numbers with Duncan on the bridge before cycling home. Giving out their numbers was against their mum's rule.

"I was hoping he would invite us in to look at his house," said Faith.

"He's only just met us. Maybe next time, he'll ask us in."

"Maybe his place is a mess and he needs to tidy up a bit," suggested Faith.

"Yeah, probably," nodded Hope knowingly.

The girls reached home and made a plan for the next fourteen days leading up to Wigtown Show. There were loads of tasks to do. More shampooing, more halter training and preparing the calves for being in a noisy environment.

And, the girls themselves had to look the part - white trousers, white shirts and a perfectly knotted tie each. Debs went online and parcels of whitish, odd sized clothes began to arrive for the girls to try on.

On day three of their hectic countdown plan the girls leaned over Blether Bridge and shouted. "Duncan! Do you want to help us at the farm today?"

"Ooh Duncan," said Max, "Those nice giwils are cawing you!"

But Duncan had already heard the call he had been longing for and was all ready and kitted out in green waterproofs and wellies. He had been sneaking up to the farm for the last few days and from an excellent hideout position on the milking parlour roof, he had been observing the show preparations. But today brought an official invitation to help. Bring it on!

Duncan grabbed his scooter and raced alongside the girls on their bikes, to the farm. When they arrived, they were unnoticed by Millie and GJ who were busy at the kitchen table which was laden with piles of paper, folders and unopened envelopes. The other farm workers were busy out in the fields on tractors and motorbikes. The farm steading, much to Duncan's joy, was deserted of humans. This meant he could really get stuck in helping!

Duncan began by demonstrating his cowboy tricks by skilfully lassooing halters onto the calves.

"How did you do that?" asked Hope in admiration.

"Skill - practice makes perfect," Duncan replied simply.

Duncan then took both halters that were attached to the calves and began leading them around the farm steading effortlessly.

Faith was quite disgruntled at this. "We have been trying to get them to walk like this for days and then he turns up, with no experience and the calves behave beautifully...I just don't get it!"

"I do," said Hope. "Look at his eyes. The calves are making eye contact with him. We have been so busy watching their feet we didn't look them in the eyes."

"Duncan, this is fantastic,"

praised Hope. The next thing we need to prepare them for is the noise of the show at Wigtown."

"GJ thinks playing Radio 2 in the parked tractor in the steading with the door open, is ample preparation," added Faith. "But it's always Scottish music being played at the show, we need some Scottish music."

Duncan immediately produced his i-pod. Within seconds, rousing Scottish ceilidh music filled the steading. The calves perked up their ears and began dancing Scottish country dances in perfect dressage pony style.

After that, the calves were so exhausted, they were relieved to have their halters on and do exactly as they were told. But the dances they had performed were not to be forgotten.

Then there was an uneasy moment when they heard Millie calling them. In a nimble flash, Duncan legged it up a drainpipe and onto the milking parlour roof.

"Hi girls!" callled Millie. Come and have some juice and cake. It's carrot cake today."

Millie's cake were legendary for the wrong reasons. Millie's cakes were either crisply burnt and as dry as sand or they were undercooked with runny eggs scooshing out when you took a bite. (Fortunately Roxy the Jack Russell Terrier didn't care what their texture should have been.)

They followed Millie into the kitchen where GJ sat at the table muttering into piles of blank forms and unpaid bills. He glanced up briefly,"Harrumphehh."

Unknown to the girls, Duncan had invited himself into the house too. He had nipped into Millie's utility room and had settled himself in the laden clothes pulley turned troll hammock. The utility room was next to the kitchen so he could see and hear all that was going on.

Roxy spied the cake being sliced. The girls loved carrot cake, but Millie's one appeared to contain suspiciously raw looking, chunkily chopped, unpeeled carrots and runny eggs. Roxy licked her lips. Duncan licked his lips; a little too loudly. Roxy growled and trotted into the utility room to investigate. Millie poured out glasses of orange juice, her thoughts elsewhere as usual.

After a few sniffs, Roxy located Duncan. Her coat bristled, her ears stood to attention and her teeth were on show as she snarled and gazed up at Duncan, who was looking very comfortable in his latest hideout.

"Roxy! Come and see what I've got! Faith called, desperate to get rid of her cake.

"Dinnaebefeedinthedug," grouched GJ.

"Faith, he says you've not to feed Roxy," Hope warned.

But Roxy wasn't interested anyway, as she continued to snarl savagely (which was out of character). Afraid that Roxy would blow his cover, in one slick movement, Duncan swung on the pulley as hard as he could. All the wet laundry tipped over the startled

dog while
Duncan
escaped
past the
temporarily
blind Roxy

and went back to his lookout to wait
for the girls. The girls sniggered as
Roxy staggered back to the kitchen
wearing a pink frilly bra over her
head and a pair of grey holey boxer
shorts over her tail. Meanwhile, back
on the roof, Duncan waited
impatiently.

Soon Millie and the girls were
back outside. Millie thanked the girls
and turned to go back into the
house. When the coast was clear,
Duncan leapt from the roof and
landed perfectly on the scooter Faith
was holding for him. The girls
retrieved the slices of carrot cake

from their hiding places and gave them to Duncan who munched them happily as they cycled and scooted back to their homes.

Chapter Six

Duncan had always thought the neighbouring farm to GJ's appeared much more exciting than GJ's place. There were masses of massive machines there. Huge tractors, harvesters, balers, ploughs, mowers, drills, silage trailers, muck spreaders and Duncan's most favourite one of all, the forager with big scary eyes painted on it! Sometimes they came and worked on GJ's fields and Duncan would find a good hiding spot and watch them toil away for hours. One day he even hoped to travel aboard one of them.

But even better than the machinery, were the horses and ponies. Duncan's favourite one was called Dandy and belonged to the farmer's daughter, Lucy. And he was about to become a very handy Dandy as part of Duncan's clever plan to get to Wigtown Show.

His plan involved reaching the farm steading on show morning by becoming a stowaway on the farm quad bike when Sam the dairyman was bringing in the cows for milking. He would then jump into the boot of Millie's Range Rover and wait for Hope, Faith and Millie.

But Duncan had a slight problem with the quad bike part of the plan. Duncan's balance was not terrific. (He had discovered this when learning to ride his scooter - it had taken him months of persevering to be able to stay on.) So while Lucy was at school, Duncan decided he was going to teach himself how to ride Dandy, in order to improve his balancing skills.

There was only a field separating Duncan's bridge from Dandy's field. It was too bumpy to scoot there so he had to trudge his way uphill and was quite puffed out when he arrived for his first DIY riding lesson. However he did look the part, he thought, wearing a red velvet cowboy hat and a spotty bandana he had found in Millie's bin.

When he got to Dandy's field, the pony eyed him up suspiciously. Duncan's first problem was how to mount Dandy. He looked around the field for a solution. Bingo! Lucy's trampoline had been blown from the garden into the field during a stormy night. All he needed to do was to lure

Dandy to stand near the trampoline. He had watched Lucy entice Dandy with Granny Smith apples, so he had hinted to Hope and Faith they were his favourites and they had brought him a big bag full of them. He swaggered past Dandy and took a cheeky bite out of one of the apples then waved it under Dandy's nostrils teasingly. Dandy fell for the bait and followed the wylie troll to the trampoline. Duncan then placed the rest of the apples on the ground beside the trampoline.

Next he clambered onto the trampoline and began to bounce. His first attempt to land on Dandy's back failed... as did all his attempts for the first twenty minutes. Many would have given up at this stage, but Duncan NEVER gave up with anything he was attempting to achieve; no matter how long it took.

Just as the apples were beginning to run out, his final attempt was a

success and he landed perfectly in the centre of Dandy's back. Well almost perfectly. Duncan was facing Dandy's tail instead of his head, but after a very clumsy manoeuvre, he was able to grip Dandy's mane and swivel awkwardly round to face the right way. Dandy snorted. Duncan had often watched Lucy riding and she seemed to kick Dandy in the sides to get him moving. He stretched out his legs as far as he could on either side of Dandy, then walloped them into the poor pony's sides as hard as he could muster. Well that was it! Dandy was off round the field like a racehorse at the Grand National.

For a few seconds Duncan bobbed up and down, his backside flying into the air, way above Dandy's back. Then Duncan was off...literally. He was thrown several metres in the air before landing slap bang in one of Dandy's recent poos. Duncan was sure Dandy was smiling as he stood watching. He scowled at Dandy, went to his water trough and washed his waterproofs in his drinking water.

"Apologise," said Dandy.

"Me, apologise?" asked Duncan, a bit startled, "You deliberately threw me into your dung."

"Yes, you apologise," answered Dandy, "First you try to ride me without even asking me, then you kick me far too hard and now you have dirtied up my water."

Duncan considered this request for a few seconds. "Well if I apologise, will you let me ride on your back again?"

"Might do. Depends on how good your apology is," said Dandy.

"OK, I'm sorry. I didn't know ponies could speak so I didn't ask your permission. I was only trying to copy Lucy when I kicked you and I used your water in a temper. Sorry."

"Apology accepted. Now get back on and I'll talk you through what to do," Dandy said, quite amused by this unusual character.

"Much obwiged," thanked Duncan, using the polite phrase Max had taught him.

Dandy lay down and Duncan hopped on his back. Dandy stood up slowly and then walked gently round the field allowing Duncan to get used to balancing on him.

"Woo hoo! This is fun!" yelled Duncan. "What a view! I can see the park and the school and the sea and the Isle of Man! This is awesome!"

However, after a while, they could also see Lucy's mum standing on the patio with her hands on her hips and a slightly puzzled look on her face.

"Best call it a day for now," said Dandy, "come back tomorrow and we can try some trotting." He lay down to let Duncan dismount. Duncan thanked Dandy, gave his head a friendly stroke and headed back home, daydreaming of adventures on horseback.

Chapter Seven

The day before Wigtown Show was manic panic. Everyone was on board to ensure the calves' appearance at the show was a success. The calves were repeatedly bathed in their coconut shampoo and even GJ agreed they were looking, 'not bad,' which Millie assured the girls, was a huge compliment.

Dandy had kept his promise and had taught Duncan to ride every day for the past week until they were confident Duncan's balancing skills were up to performing stunt tricks on the farm quad bike on show morning.

Millie's many friends arrived to place food and drinks in her fridges for the annual after show barbecue. Millie made a picnic lunch and placed it in the Range Rover's boot.

GJ sent some men to the show field with tarpaulins to place over the

calves' stand to protect them from the gloriously hot sun's rays that were forecast.

Hope and Faith packed the battered wooden show box with all the paperwork and calf kit they required.

Everyone went to bed early, but it was like trying to get to sleep on Christmas Eve.

Chapter Eight

After what felt like the fastest of sleeps, the morning of Wigtown Show opened its sleepy curtains.

Max had not slept well. Under strict instructions from Duncan, he had to alert him immediately when the lights flicked on in the farmhouse. Duncan's plan was ridiculously simple. Once the farmhouse lights were on, he would trundle into the cow field and find Lulu. The cows at the farm liked to meander to the milking parlour in the same order every day. Lulu liked to be last. Always. Every single morning, Lulu was determined to be the last cow in the milky line up.

So every morning, Sam, the sleepy dairyman, had to ride the quad bike right up close to Lulu, to wake her up and guide her to follow the herd out of the field into the farm steading.

So at five o'clock on show morning, it was not quite light when Duncan heard, "The wights a on, Duncy, it's time to get up."

Duncan was a morning person, so he jumped out of bed, carefully put on the clothes he had laid out the night before and headed off.

He crawled through the hedge

into Lulu's field. Lulu was easy to recognise; she was the only cow still asleep and had a cute black upside down triangle on her white face. Duncan cuddled down close to her to keep warm. The faint roar of the ancient quad bike was soon heard approaching.

Lulu opened one eye and ignored Sam's wake up call. "Just five more minutes," she whispered.

Unable to persuade Lulu onto her feet after much tooting of the quad bike horn, Sam hopped off the motorbike. He gave Lulu a friendly pat on the side to tell her that her snooze button was activated.

As Sam hopped off the motorbike, Duncan hopped on. In one slick Commonwealth Games hurdle style movement, Duncan threw himself onto the quad bike. When Sam jumped back on, Duncan clung onto Sam's cow stinking jacket and began to bump along the field behind Lulu and the herd. Sam's driving was awesome; white knuckle ride stuff. Thank goodness for Dandy's lessons thought Duncan, as his hands gripped Sam's jacket and his legs flew out in a straight line behind him. Forget Alton Towers, he thought as he tried not to yell "Weeeheee!" out loud.

When they reached the farm steading, Duncan was startled when Sam suddenly stopped the bike and leaving the engine running, he jumped off. He seemed to be heading to the open gate they had just driven through. Duncan was now completely visible to anyone who happened to be around at half past five in the morning. He was also capable of giving young Sam an early heart attack if he looked round at any moment. But Sam was engrossed and muttering at the frayed binder twine he was using to secure the old rusty gate shut.

Duncan sniffed a moment of mischief. He clambered onto the saddle of the motorbike, hopped onto the footplate and made his escape to hide behind a very obliging old oil drum. He continued to sniff the mischief opportunity. Sam, who had been playing computer games far too late the night before, was still fumbling with the frayed binder twine and trying to secure the gate. Duncan had spied a horn icon on the bike as he was getting off...

With speed he didn't know existed, Duncan shot back onto the bike, found the horn and...toot toot to toot toot toot toot! As Sam was turning round in shock and disbelief, Duncan was haring back to his oil drum hiding place.

Now Sam had heard the expression many times before. Fortunately he had never experienced it. Until now. Sam had got such a fright, he had pooed his pants.

Chapter Nine

Duncan headed to the machinery
shed and stood behind the cattle
trailer that was already attached to
Millie's top of the range, Range
Rover. He stripped off his waterproof
trousers and jacket to reveal his
outfit of trendy shorts and t-shirt. He
replaced his wellies with extremely
trendy trainers and lastly popped his
baseball cap on. He hid his
discarded clothes behind an oil
drum, jumped into the jeep and
waited. After a while he became a bit
bored in the back seat, so he climbed
into the driver's seat and pretended
he was driving and began spinning
the steering wheel wildly. Then he
noticed Millie had left the keys in the

ignition. Duncan hoped that one tiny turn of the key would not cause any serious harm. Luckily for him, all it did was activate some of the electric features. He started with the windscreen wipers, followed by the hazard lights and finally the electric windows. The car was alive! He turned on the CD player and began to move like Jagger.

Unfortunately he didn't get to dance to the end of the song, as Hope and Faith walked into the shed laden with show stuff. Duncan abandoned his driver's seat dancing podium and leap frogged into the boot.

Hope and Faith looked at one another. There was only one character who could be responsible.

"Ooh!" exclaimed Millie, "Even the

Range Rover's excited about going to the show," and she opened the boot and threw in a basket with last minute essential drinks and sun lotion.

As the girls loaded the calves into the trailer, Millie got into the driver's seat and switched off all Duncan's playthings, except for the CD player.

"Good job she is so dizzy," Faith whispered, as Tilly and Primrose sauntered into the cattle trailer like they had practised.

"You don't think for a minute Duncan is still in the Range Rover?" asked Hope as they walked towards it.

Right on cue, a smiling, jubilant figure in a baseball cap gave them the thumbs up from the back window.

"Oh. My. Giddy. Aunt," was all Hope managed as Millie tooted the horn to hurry them on.

Millie talked non stop on the ten minute journey to the show. "You must be nervous girls. I have never known you two to be so quiet - especially you Faith! Now don't be nervous - you have absolutely nothing to worry about," she giggled.

The girls exchanged screwed up facial expressions. They had mega worries.

Meanwhile Duncan was enjoying a lush breakfast. Crisps, thickly buttered tattie scones and two Seriously Strong cheese salad rolls washed down with half a flask of hot, milky tea.

Breakfast over, Duncan keeked out and shook with delight. Wigtown

Show! He was about to achieve one of his lifelong ambitions by attending Wigtown Show. The early morning sun glistened down on the great spectacle of machinery stands, funfair rides, rows and rows of livestock pens and white tents of all sizes. Duncan was almost sick with excitement.

He then looked over at Faith and wondered why she was pulling a Balaclava over her head. Surely bank robbing before the show wasn't Millie's latest money making idea?

It was the standard joke that all the children covered their faces in embarrassment when Millie towed the horsebox. Forwards, fine, backwards; well, that was never going to happen smoothly,

Millie hurtled along the gravel

entrance to the show at a Schumacher pace that sent dust and gravel flying. Millie was oblivious. Her Range Rover skidded to a happy halt.

Hope had opened the glove box containing their parking disguises. Wigs, hats, sun glasses and false moustaches were offered so the girls would not be recognised later and be teased about their incompetent driver. Millie was too busy concentrating to notice the costume changes.

Duncan soon realised the need for the disguises. Millie's reverse parking of a vehicle and trailer was not fancy.

After fifteen minutes of Hope and Faith's, "Right a bit. Left a bit. No too far. Yes now, straighten up. Left hand down on steering wheel. No left hand..." a queue was beginning to form behind the giggling Millie. Eventually, the president of the show saw the traffic jam and kindly and expertly parked Millie's Range Rover and trailer for her.

The girls threw off their disguises and rushed round to the trailer to get the calves out. As Millie and the girls led the calves to their stand, Duncan jumped out of the boot and sneaked into the trailer. A wheelbarrow full of inviting straw became his next hiding place. He hopped in and dived below the straw, just as Hope came back to empty the rest of the trailer out. She grabbed the wheelbarrow.

"OK. The game's up. I know you're in here. I am going to put you in the wooden show box, leave the lid a little open so you can breathe, and you are going to stay there for the rest of the day, you annoying little man," she hissed. "I thought you didn't want spotted and captured? There are thousands of people here! Are you mad?"

Not as mad as you are, thought Duncan, as he smiled weakly and nodded at Hope. When they reached their stand, Faith and Millie were fussing with the calves as Hope emptied the contents of the show box, then roughly tipped Duncan and some more stuff in. She propped the lid open with a plastic box full of sausage rolls.

"I mean it. Stay put. There are journalists, TV crews and plenty of pens and cages here for them to put you in," she warned.

As Hope went over and whispered to Faith, and Faith turned to look at the show box, Duncan shuddered at the thought of a televised capture. However there was no way he was staying in this troll coffin for the rest of the day! He munched his way through the sausage rolls while he came up with a plan. All his efforts to get here were not going to be wasted. No way.

Chapter Ten

As Millie, Hope and Faith took the
calves for yet another bath, Duncan
made his escape. It was still very
early and only people with stands
and stalls were about. They were all
engrossed in preparing for the public
to arrive. So Duncan went for a
dander. He ducked and dived his
way round the cattle stands followed
by the sheep stands. There really
were some interesting looking cows
and sheep at the show. Then in the
distance he saw the bouncy castle
slide. At this time of day, he could
have it all to himself! So off he
slinked towards it, dodging in and
out of animal stands and pens
having enormous fun tickling

unsuspecting animals on his way, until...

Duncan turned a corner, and there before him, stood dozens of them - the dreaded, the awful, the enemy. Goats.

Just like Max the otter liked to claim he was a descendant of Mij of Ring of Bright Water fame, Duncan also claimed to have a famous ancestor.

Duncan liked to boast to Max that his ancestor was that very troll from the Three Billy Goats Gruff Story. Now, because of what happened to that tricked troll in that story, all trolls, all over the world, have an inbuilt loathing of goats. Any goats. Any breed, any size, any shape. All goats, anywhere, everywhere. Trolls hate goats, full stop.

Duncan was bursting to reveal his anger at the cheek of goats. Goats attending, parading and strutting their stuff at Wigtown Show. These impudent goats are jeering at me he thought and wondered if they were beginning to plot how they could repeat history by closing in on him and butting him out of the show field.

Think positive, thought Duncan. Turn this situation around. Use it to your advantage. The goats continued to sneer and giggle. But Duncan sneered back. He had a cunning plan.

At all agricultural shows there are lots of trade stands and Wigtown show liked to boast that it had 'something for everyone.'

This meant there were always

sweet stalls, toy stalls and better still, toys that sold practical jokes! Stink bombs, fart sprays, plastic poos and silly string and brightly coloured hair sprays...

Silly string and fluorescent hair sprays, thought Duncan. Just like Tilly and Primrose, the goats had endured hours and hours of washing, cleaning and grooming from their proud, hard working, decent goat owners. Sneering, smirking, smug goats. Flourescent pink highlights punctuated with messy, sticky silly string decorations...Oh yes, thought Duncan. Perfect revenge from the troll world to the goat world.

The gates had now opened to the public, so sneaking through the rapidly building throng of show goers, Duncan expertly launched himself onto the under seat basket of a passing toddler's buggy. As he was shoogled along, he had a rummage in his makeshift taxi. There was a rather nice navy quilted jacket, a plastic feeding cup with far too weak blackcurrant juice in it and a bag of 'Hyper' sweeties. "Mmmm," chewed Duncan.

The unsuspecting harassed mum was hopefully heading in the direction of the children's area in order to shut up the squawking brat of an older child that she was dragging at a 45 degree angle.

As luck would have it, Duncan could see the bouncy castle approaching. Now the only experience Duncan had of women were the dippy ones in his opinion.

Debs? Duh? Millie...double Duh? Duncan was worried that the Wigtown Show secretary, who was a woman, would not have the sense to place the bouncy castles near the children's stands.

Duncan stood corrected. The Wigtown Show secretary had played a blinder! The dazzling area designed for children's entertainment was spectacular! Thanks to her intelligence, he was certain the hairspray and string were within easy reach.

He was not disappointed. As he leapt from his taxi, Duncan bounded towards a stall where a very attractive, smartly dressed, well spoken lady was checking that the stall holder was not selling any items that could be used to make a sudden noise and scare any animals. She then announced to the growingly grumpy stall holder that she may not sell items that would offend show goers. Much to his disappointment Duncan watched her remove the spray fart cans from her stand but was relieved to see the hairsprays and silly string remained there.

The efficient secretary left the stallholder muttering about removing the spray fart cans and Duncan saw this as his cue to make a move.

In an instant he was under her stall and squeezing his teeth into her ankles. Like a child biting into that horrible paste the orthodontist uses, he sank his sharp little teeth in as far as he could. As she squealed and leapt and thrashed about in pain to the astonishment of all the families around, she crashed over her stall, sending crisps, sweets, drink cans, inflatable hammers, plastic poos and midget gems flying in all directions. Cans of silly string and coloured hairsprays carpeted the grass beneath the stand.

Result, thought Duncan as he expertly stuffed the cans of hairspray and string into a carrier bag that was lying on the ground. Greedily he also snatched a fake poo that he was sure would come in handy some day. And off he went, leaving behind a scene of utter chaos.

Within minutes, Duncan was back with the goats, thanks to another buggy basket taxi. He even managed to catch an express buggy on his return journey as the dad was jogging towards the Portaloo with a desperate three year old.

When he reached the first goat stand, Duncan jumped off the speeding buggy, clamboured up the end pole of the goats' stand and slid onto the tarpaulin that was sheltering them.

Lying on his tummy, he poked his head over the edge of the tarpaulin. With a can of silly string in one hand and pink fluorescent hairspray in the other, he took careful aim over his first goat victim.

"Ploouch!" went the green silly string. "Squwoosh!" squirted the hairspary. The goat looked up, startled.

"Cool!" bleated the goat next to it. As Duncan squirted merrily away, the goats lapped up their new

treatments.
This was not
the reaction
he had been
expecting.
He stopped
suddenly,
realising he
was wasting

his time. These stupid goats were
enjoying their pampering! Spying a
bucket of water beside the goats,
Duncan jumped down and tossed
the water all over the two goats,
leaving them both in a gooey, sticky
mess.

The goats were furious.
Neighbouring goats smirked. Duncan
looked around to check the goat
handlers were still busy chatting. He
squirted more hairspray and silly
string onto the neighbouring

goats and just as he was about to soak them with water, he heard the yell of one of the goat handlers.

"Aaggghhh!" she yelled. "My goats!"

As Duncan attempted to make a speedy exit, he bumped straight into the biggest goat in the show. Before he had time to speak or take a breath, he felt himself rising and rising as he was tossed into the air by the huge goats' horns. Higher and higher he soared, above the goats, above the tractor stands, over the bouncy castles, twirling, swirling, just like one of his firework farts.

Duncan actually enjoyed his travel through space over the show field. After the initial surprise of the goat butt, (there was no pain, as trolls don't experience pain), he cackled to himself in delight as he spun forwards at what seemed like one hundred miles per hour towards the horse show jumping area.

Chapter Eleven

"Oops sorry!" he apologised, as he landed with a splat in a soft pile of hay, next to a had been asleep cute little girl. Emma Bea smiled at him sleepily, "That's OK, I was just having a quick nap. I'm Emma, Emma Bea."

"I'm Duncan. And actually, I'm feeling a bit sick..."

Just in time, Emma Bea picked up her riding hat

that was sitting next to her and held it out to catch Duncan's lengthy, noisy vomit.

"I am sooo sorry! How embarrassing! I have only just met you and I have just puked my chocolate sickness into your lovely hat! I can't believe what I have just done…"

"Chocolate?" sniffed Emma, "Wow!"

"Oh yes, always chocolate. Milk, white, with bubbles, mint flavoured…just depends what I've been eating lately," Duncan explained. "Would you care to sample some?"

"Oh yes please!" said Emma.

Duncan then obligingly provided Emma with the tools she required to dunk in the chocolate. He pressed one of his stubby little fingers against one nostril, closed his eyes and concentrated. Out of the open nostril began to emerge a delicious looking thick marshmallow stick, in pretty, striped, pastel colours. When it was out and grasped in Duncan's other hand, he broke it in two and gave Emma Bea one half. He dipped his half in the riding hat chocolate and then slurped the chocolate off appreciatively.

Duncan's snotters were marshmallows. His vomit was chocolate. His farts were fireworks. He really was one very cool troll.

As Duncan and Emma Bea dunked and chatted, Duncan discovered that Emma Bea and her family were going to Millie's barbecue later on. Excitedly, they hatched a secret plan to meet up at Millie's house.

Duncan left Emma Bea to get back to her pony and wondered where he could explore next. He slinked his way around the horses and horse boxes cautiously. Looking for his next taxi to appear, he jumped with glee as he saw a miniature train coming towards him!

Better still, the back carriages were vacant and it was an easy hop for him to get on board. He crouched down, peeked over the edge of his carriage and enjoyed the most amazing tour of the show field. He spent ages taking in all the sights and sounds, until the train jolted to a halt in front of a large, white, important looking marquee.

As Duncan noticed lots of new

passengers approaching the train, he had to make a quick exit over the side of his carriage and into the basket of a luxury double buggy, being steered towards the important looking marquee.

Duncan had no idea what or who was in the marquee, so he was even more excited about his next Wigtown Show experience. He did not realise that this was the poultry marquee and that this year's VIP royal guest was inside being shown around.

As the buggy entered the jam packed marquee, Duncan froze with terror. Cages! His worst nightmare! He looked inside the cages and saw chickens, geese, ducks and lots of exotic versions of them, caged up for people to ogle at and admire. These poor innocent birds, thought Duncan. This was scandalous!

Luckily, the buggy driver was now up close to a line of cages. So Duncan did what he thought was the right thing to do. He leaned over and began to unclip the latch of each cage as the buggy passed down the line of cages. As the buggy driver chatted with her toddler about 'the pretty birdies' she was unaware that she was transporting a troll on a mission.

Chapter Twelve

It actually took the first few birds a few moments to realise that their cage door had been opened, but when they did realise, the result was a domino effect. One by one each bird escaped. They flapped their wings, they danced, they scurried about and seemed to sense the mischief that Duncan had caused. Within ten minutes, the marquee was in chaos. There were birds and feathers and bird poo flying in all directions. The show secretary was trying to usher out the VIP royal guest and apologise for the

uproar, but the VIP royal guest
actually looked quite amused.

Now news travels very fast in the
Wigtown area and it was not long
before everyone at Wigtown show
was aware that there was some kind
of a party happening in the poultry
marquee. Hoards of people were

making their way over to see what was going on and there was even a rumour that the royal VIP guest had been injured.

The show secretary was not amused. She was all too aware that someone had been causing havoc at the show. First the toy stand, then the goats and now this calamity in the poultry marquee. Swapping the Scottish music that was being played on the loudspeakers for "One way or another, I'm gonna getcha..." she marched back towards the crime scene.

News also travels fast within the livestock world at Wigtown Show and nobody likes to miss a good party. By the time the irate secretary reached the poultry party, sheep, cows,calves, dogs and goats had broken loose and were joining in the fun. The poultry marquee was the place to be. It was a blast; a circus of excited farm animals all showing off together.

Meanwhile, Duncan was huddled in the buggy basket, realising the havoc he had caused and also discovering for the first time, that he had a fear of feathers as well as cages. He was about to panic just as he saw bright daylight as the buggy was driven out of the marquee and back into the show field.

Duncan urgently needed a hiding place. He scoured the corner of the show field he had escaped to for any potential locations...Bingo!

An empty bus sat with its engine running. Empty, apart from Andy the secret millionaire bus driver who was engrossed in his phone. Duncan recognised Andy's bus as the one that sat outside the village school every day at 3 o'clock. He had cheekily hopped on it one day in the village square when he had been laden with some bin hoking shopping. The wee trip from the village square to the school had saved him walking a good bit of the journey home.

Duncan hopped up the bus steps, slinked past an oblivious Andy and chose a comfortable abandoned jacket under seat number 14 to snuggle into. He reached into the jacket's pocket in the hope of discovering a wee snack and finding pickled onion crisps, he began to munch. He began to munch just a wee bit too noisily. Andy looked up from his phone with a puzzled look on his face.

He half listened and half kept an eye on his phone. Because Andy was one of the few millionaire bachelors in the area, he was always inundated with messages from ladies claiming to be his perfect match. In fact on the last leap year day, Andy had to enlist help opening his fan mail which was full of marriage proposals. Poor Andy, he was a lovely natured soul and his friends hoped he was able to sort out his genuine admirers from the gold diggers!

So Duncan munched as Andy scrolled through his messages. It was only when Duncan let out a massive burp that Andy threw his precious phone to the floor and stood up in utter shock.

Duncan reckoned he had four choices. Phone a friend. Escape out the bus fire exit, try to stay hidden or and it was very big risky or, befriend Andy...

Andy was standing up now with a half nervous smile on his face, "Right, come on, which one of you kids is hiding in here? You lot are always playing tricks on me," he called with a nervous laugh.

Duncan stayed hidden under the jacket under seat number 14. He began to think hard. The day he had sneaked a lift on Andy's bus, he had noticed how well all the children on the bus got on with Andy. They laughed and joked and shared their sweets with him. Befriending a bus driver might not be such a bad thing and this one was child friendly so he might be prepared to be troll friendly too. Unlimited bus access could lead to all sorts of new opportunities.

He could go shopping in new destinations. He could see a bit of the world and he knew that Andy even went to the city sometimes to watch football matches and stay in posh hotels.

"Right, where are you? I bet it's you Gregor," you wee monkey.

In his boldest voice, Duncan keeked out from

under the jacket and shouted indignantly, "I am not Gregor and I am certainly **not** a mmmonkey!"

Now Andy was a man of the world and he had been in some strange situations in his life and had met some strange people. However nothing could have prepared him for what he was about to encounter. He opened his mouth to speak, but nothing happened. For the first time in his life, Andy the millionaire, bachelor bus driver, was utterly speechless.

"I don't bite you know," lied Duncan as he stood up and put his hands on his hips.

"Never seen a troll before then?"

Andy's eyes grew wider and wider. His mouth gaped open as he shook his head in slow motion. Well lucky for you then that I'm a friendly, intelligent troll. It is an honour for you to meet me and I hope you appreciate that," informed Duncan. Andy's mouth remained gaping and his eyes stayed wide. The only thing that changed was the direction in which he moved his head as it went from a slow motion sideways movement to a slow disbelieving nodding.

Andy tried to speak again, but only a stammered, "Where, where, do you ..." came out.

"Where do I come from? I live under the bridge near Hope and Faith's house. Did you bring your school children to the show?" asked Duncan politely, now convinced how handy it would be to befriend Andy.

"No," managed Andy, then gulped and said very slowly and quietly, "I'm here to take the hen party back to the village."

"Hen party??" panicked Duncan.

Andy nodded. Immediately, Duncan shot past Andy, ran down the bus and shouted, "Must dash! Chow the now!" He flew down the bus steps and dodged and darted his way back to the cattle area. Hens! He had seen enough of those for one day.

Chapter Thirteen

As Duncan dodged towards the calves' pens, exhibitors were beginning to dismantle their stands and load up their livestock into lorries and cattle trailers.

Suddenly, a furious Hope grabbed him by the hand, threw a

picnic rug over him and dragged him along the show field.

Next he felt himself being lifted up and heard a car door slam. All had gone quiet so he peeked out from the rug to discover he was back in the boot of Millie's Range Rover. Beside him were two huge shiny trophies that the calves had obviously won. Duncan felt guilty.

It was excited chat on the way back home about the two calves winning. Millie stopped off to buy Champagne to celebrate. When she was out of the Range Rover, Hope interrupted Duncan's noshing of the last of the picnic food.

"Have you any idea of the trouble you caused today?"

"Moi?" (Max had been teaching him some French recently.)

"Don't play the innocent with me, Duncan!"

"Who else would have caused havoc at the toy stall, sabotaged goats and let dozens of caged birds loose?"

Faith spoiled Hope's serious ticking off by not being able to hold in her giggles. Her infectious chortles spluttered out. Duncan stared at Hope with his puppy dog eyes and held out his phone showing a picture of a livid goat covered in silly string.

Hope did her best to remain angry and serious; but it was useless. She began to laugh until tears were streaming down her cheeks. The more photos and videos Duncan showed them, the more they all laughed. Duncan jumped back under the picnic rug just as Millie dumped a box of bottles onto the back seat before climbing back into the driving seat.

There was just enough time for the girls to go home and get changed before they cycled to the barbecue with their mum and dad. They were a bit concerned when their mum got off her new bike at the bridge and began peering cautiously over both sides.

"What are you doing Mum?" Hope asked slightly nervously.

"Oh you know," Debs half laughed, "that silly old story about a troll living under here. I just thought I would look and see if he's about," she half laughed again.

"What a stupid story," said Hope, just a bit too quickly.

"Totally crazy," Faith mimicked, circling her index fingers at the sides of her head.

Underneath, Duncan laughed at the banter on the bridge as he prepared to party. He had managed to kit himself out for the barbecue courtesy of Lucy's mum's wheelie bin. Lucy's cousin, Gregor, was a particularly cool dude and during a recent sleepover at Lucy's, he had ditched some clothes in a ploy to get newer, trendier

ones. (His mum had fallen for the story that Lucy's mum had shrunk his stuff in the wash.) So with his new clothes, gelled hair and knowing he was back in the girls' good books, Duncan was ready and raring to go.

"Whey a you going to hide at the babecue Duncan?" asked Max.

"Up a tree, behind the bouncy castle," he replied confidently.

"Oh wow! A twee! How cwever. You'll get a gweat view fwom a twee," confirmed Max. "Have fun Dunky. Wake me up when you get back."

Chapter Fourteen

When they arrived at the farm,
Debs helped Millie light the barbecue
and prepare the food. As Hope and
Faith handed out drinks, they were
inundated with compliments about
winning the first prizes at the Show.

The party was soon in full swing
and there was great excitement as
more and more friends and
neighbours joined the celebration.
Sam was in charge of the music and
the mums danced on the patio. The
men talked about the winners and
losers at the Show and about the
price of milk.

The children bounced on the
bouncy castle or played football in
the field. Debs cooked up a storm on

the barbecue and everyone was having a great time.

Emma Bea proved to be an expert tree climber. She carried plastic plates full of burgers, sausages, chicken kebabs and sirloin steaks all drenched with fried onions, up the tree to where Duncan was perched. They happily slurped away at bottle after bottle of Irn Bru together. They talked about ponies and riding bareback and showjumping.

When the food was finished and darkness was falling, Millie climbed onto the patio table to make her speech. She popped open the Champagne and poured some into the biggest trophy and held it up proudly, although a little shakily.

"Thank you everyone for joining us tonight to celebrate winning these

marvellous trophies. Well done Hope and Faith for an epic Wigtown Show!"

Just as Millie's stiletto heel seemed to get stuck in a groove and the table began to wobble, GJ shouted, "Three cheers for the girls - Hope, Faith, Tilly and Primrose!"

As the crowd hip, hip hoorayed, Debs helped Millie get her shoe unstuck so she was able to clamber down to the patio and pass the trophy round for the grown ups to take a sip from.

Now one of the guests at the party was GJ's friend, Explosive Craig, who had earned this nickname due to his passionate ability to safely engineer public firework displays. Duncan had overheard Explosive Craig telling

Sam all about one of his latest displays when the two of them were on the bouncy castle. Impressed by Explosive Craig's knowledge and imagination, Duncan made his final plan for the day.

He waited until Explosive Craig had bounced himself dizzy and had to go and lie down in his orange camper van. Then, with Emma Bea, he jumped over the stone dyke into the field next to the garden.

Fuelled by all the extra onions Emma Bea had given him with his burgers, Duncan crouched behind a sleeping cow and he farted like his life depended on it. It was awesome!

Everyone stopped dancing and chatting to gaze at the amazing fireworks.

"GanonyerselCraig!" yelled GJ.

"Go for it Craig!" translated Millie.

The crowd applauded and cheered when the display was finally over, before returning to their chatting or dancing. Everyone, except Debs. Debs continued to look at the field, then at a fast asleep Craig in his camper van.

The party continued into the wee small hours. Duncan was too exhausted to scoot home so he left his scooter beside the camper van and got a taxi ride home on the back of Hope's bike.

"Ooh that thounded good fun Dunky," welcomed Max.

Duncan nodded wearily, snuggled into bed and drifted off into a deep and imaginative mischief filled sleep, reflecting on all the adventurous new friends he had made. All thanks to Wigtown Show.